The Feu Follet

Cara Lyons Legé

Cara Lyons Legé

PublishAmerica

Baltimore

First printing

ISBN: 1-59286-262-4
PUBLISHED BY PUBLISHAMERICA BOOK
PUBLISHERS
www.publishamerica.com
Baltimore

Printed in the United States of America

Dedicated to
My Beloved Daughter
Marty Lynn Legé
(Maury)

ACKNOWLEGEMENTS

There really is a Kimball farm.
Maury and Kevin did share part of their lives together there.

I want to thank the Kimballs for allowing me to use their names in this book. And for sharing their home and spirit with all the Kimball riders during those years we were together.

I acknowledge the contributions of my daughter, Maury, for telling me stories about the farm, as she remembered them.

I tried to capture the images and feel and growing pains of those pre-teen years.

However, this is a fictional tale, not a biography.

She reached down and rolled the boiled frog over with a stick. There was nothing to guess about – she knew that the dead thing was a warning, a warning for Kevin to leave this house.

Chapter One

Maury

Maury was twelve years old and her world was falling down.

For someone who was used to life going pretty much as she wanted it to, it was hard to believe that she was in the middle of an uproar that she probably brought on herself.

When she moved her horse to the Kimball Farm, everything was supposed to be perfect. And it was, until today.

She had seen the boiled frog all right. There it was,

lying plain as day, pink belly up, under Kevin's back porch. She knew straight away that the frog was a voodoo symbol. Right then, right there, things went from bad to worse.

There was no way out of this hole she dug for herself. And two nights ago Kevin had almost been hurt because of her.

She looked at him as he walked down the Kimball's front steps. He looked tired. So was she. After the troubling conversations they had been having, it was no wonder that neither of them had gotten a good night's sleep. And now this!

She thought, "Once we've talked it over, we'll feel better. Sure, that was it, sure we will."

It was cold that morning. Maury pulled her down-filled vest tight around her chest and leaned back on the trunk of the sprawling oak in the Kimball's front yard. A bone-chilling wind sprang up, shaking dry leaves from the oak.

Without meaning to, she heard the argument between the Kimball brothers. It was more chilling than the wind.

"Well?" Craig Kimball said, shaking his head in disgust.

"Well, what?" his older brother, Kevin, answered.

"Well, what's happening, Kevin? I know all this weird stuff going on around here is your fault."

Kevin didn't answer, but turned on his heels and stormed off toward the barn.

"Kevin, wait," Maury called, hurrying after him.

He turned and held up his hand to stop her. "Don't say anything else, Maury. It's no use."

She stuffed her hands in her pockets and a knowing silence fell between them.

Hadn't they known? She and Kevin?

Something was bound to happen.

Kevin walked away and Maury stumbled as she turned to look down at the dead thing.

While everyone else scrambled around muttering and scaring themselves to death, Maury was silent, her head spinning. She didn't want to think anymore.

The truth was that she was afraid they would find out about her role in it. She slipped away.

Maury couldn't go back and she couldn't move forward until she made things right again. She didn't know, quite yet, how to arrange it. But she knew it was time to do something, to have a talk with Lapin, before things got worse. She wheeled around, snapped out of those drifting thoughts, and got in motion.

It didn't take her long to tack up. And an hour later, sun on her back, she was atop her horse thinking, "Good grief, this is the worst year of my life."

She leaned back in the saddle, shading her eyes from the sun, and looked up at a perfect Louisiana sky. Low clouds hurried southeast. The familiar sound of squawking teal, returning to the rice fields nudged her out of her thoughts, and startled Blue Chip.

With one hand resting on the pommel, Maury learned over and rubbed Chip's thick gray neck.

"Easy, boy," she said, looking across the fields at the unpaved lane that disappeared into the woods beyond, "not much further to go." They ambled on at a slow pace, giving Maury time to think.

Tucked back in those trees was Lapin's house. Maury

was on her way there to get to the bottom of things.

She had gotten an early start. The early autumn breeze was unusually cold, blowing away the hot winds of summer and rattling the scarlet-tipped sugar cane in the Kimball's small acreage.

In another month, the songs of the cane fields would begin, the fields crowded with cane carts and harvesters. Then would come the burning of the fields, and soon after, a cold snowless winter.

But right now Maury was free to be by herself and give in to that rush she always felt when she gazed around at her homeland.

She breathed in the cane-sweetened air and sat a little straighter in the saddle. .

As she rode down a canebrake, Maury silently sorted out the things that had happened these past weeks, certain that somehow she had caused them.

She wished that she could put it out of her mind and let it drop, but it was too late for wishful thinking now.

Let's back up.

* * * *

When she wasn't on her horse, Maury always had her feet planted firmly on the ground. So the strange things that started happening at the Kimball farm that September hadn't scared her as much as they had the other riders. She knew how people could get worked up. And she didn't have much sympathy for people who believed in spooks and ghosts. But when a riptide of gossip spread through the farm about voodoo spells and gris gris dolls, and things got crazier Maury was less and less sure of things. Being unsure of things was a new feeling for her.

It seemed eerie out here, even in the clear morning air, as she thought back to the rainy afternoon Mamere, Lapin's great aunt, warned her about conjure balls and talismans, good luck and bad luck. And someone putting a spell on you!

Maury shuttered remembering her shrugged response to the warnings. "Yeah, well. Whatever."

She tried to remember more of what was said that day, while an uneasy feeling kept growing inside of her.

Maury knew a lot about the bayou country. She'd lived all her life in this gray misty place, where fog hangs over the marsh and drifts down between the cypress trees. And stifling heat rises on a breeze so slight that it barely stirs the beards of Spanish moss tumbling from the limbs of the great oaks.

She knew where the honeysuckle and blackberries grew. She knew where to find the furry animals taking cover in the bitter weeds and marsh grasses.

There was music in the marsh, the base of the great frogs and high shrill of crickets.

Maury's dad, who was happiest in his khaki trail clothes, and was a hunter himself, cautioned her about early rising shooters, who downed coffee, and headed to their hiding places. There they'd begin the game played year after year between themselves and migrating water foul.

Hunters ranked low on Maury's scale - these people

who stalk or lie in wait in the scrubby bottomland, hunting until the sun rose above the tree line. They were the only things she feared in the marsh.

These hunters came in increasing number, upsetting the delicate balance in the coastal waters. With them came gunshots.

Circling down in blissful ignorance, mallards, feathers purple and green; and pintails skimming through the trees, brought down on the cold winds from the north, were always in someone's gun sight.

It was wonderful in the full light of day, walking in the sunshine, leaves crunching underfoot, stirrings coming from every tree.

But at the end of the day, in the creeping shadows and dying light, the wind moaned louder. With only the dim light of the moon in the mist, everything turned to shades of gray. Cypress trees watched silently, arms outstretched, beckoning you closer. Wheel around and you might be caught like Spanish moss, in the spidery branches.

Then the morning sun restored the beauty and colors of the wind stirred trees, whose arms weren't grabbling, but merely interlacing overhead.

Though she was never known to be faint-hearted, even Maury knew about poisonous plants and crawling creatures lurking in the gray silent shadows. Green parasitic things, glad for their own lives, could climb and strangle life from weakened dying trees.

The marsh was off limits to the younger kids, and they were afraid to go in anyway.

Little Ashley Bell always said, "This place gives me

the willies. Reminds me of a graveyard." She had never forgotten seeing a snake wrapped around a raccoon, squeezing its life away.

Maury never admitted that she was afraid. She learned nature's secrets quickly, asking and observing. She believed with certainty that the bayou seemed to beckon her to hear its secrets. After all, she had been riding in and around these lowlands since she was three years old.

The grass on their marshy flats was perfect for the grazing of horses and cattle. It was made sweet and green by Louisiana rains. Not a fine misty rain, but heavy drenching rains pinging the windows, and streaming down the pains.

Sometimes, at night the rain drummed so steadily that Maury couldn't stop listening to its muffled hammering, pounding the roof. Rain that kept her inside, curtains drawn, friendly lamp lit, while she snuggled under her covers, and the world outside her window disappeared.

Chapter Two

Lapin

The Hurst Riding Stables were near a wooded area twelve miles west of Maury's home. When she moved her new Tennessee Walker to the stable, she met Lapin, and the sixth grade would never be the same again - for either of them. Just in the way that unplanned things happen, they were to begin a strange adventure.

Lapin was a Cajun girl, whose ancestors were French fur trappers. Their French blood mixing through the years with Spanish, Indian, and Negro, darkened her skin to olive.

Her education began in a convent school with the Carmelite nuns. But when Lapin's mother died, the nuns took her to live with Mamere, her great aunt.

She had lived so long behind the walls of the convent. And on the journey to Mamere's house, Lapin stared out of the car window, curious to see the countryside. Sunshine splashed across the windshield. It was a good sign.

Within an hour, Sister Mary Margaret turned off of the Abbeville Highway, onto Kaliste Saloom Road. Another turn and they were making their way down a winding, bumpy roadway that narrowed and grew dim. The car finally came to stop at a small cypress house on the edge of the woods.

Almost at the very moment that Lapin stepped down out of the car, Mamere, who had been waiting at the kitchen window, pushed open the screen door. Lapin stood looking around for a moment or two.

She was a quiet odd little figure, wanting to speak up and be polite, as the nuns had taught her.

But before she could speak, Mamere bounded across the porch and down the steps, scooping Lapin up in her arms.

"Give huh heah tuh me." she said, then gently placed the child down and led her inside.

Clinging to Mamere's hand, Lapin knew right away that something good was happening to her. Once inside, she found a spot on the hearthrug and was almost immediately drowsy and comfortable. It wasn't long before she dozed off in front of the afternoon fire still burning in the grate.

Watching the sleeping child, such a feeling welled up in Mamere!

Happiness had come back into her little house in size six shoes.

* * * *

Lapin awakened each morning to the sounds of Mamere banging around in the kitchen and the smell of strong coffee brewing there. Hurrying down from the attic loft, she ran into the arms of the one she loved most in the world.

Lapin's veins were filled with the blood of her ancestors. She heard them whispering in her ears, giving her the certain feeling that she could see things that others could not see, and hear things that others could not hear.

She roamed alone through the bayou, and mostly liked it that way. As it was with other children who didn't have brothers and sisters, she learned to play by herself. And the discipline of the convent had prepared her for making the best of a situation.

As the weeks passed, however, she thought more and more about old friends at the convent school.

Lapin couldn't find her way with new kids. She circled around them, never fitting in. Or she angered too quickly, pushing them further away, wondering how the others seem to find the middle so easily.

Lapin had to walk by the Hurst Riding Stables on her way home from school everyday. She didn't stop there very often. It was usually filled with girls from Lafayette, heads thrown back, laughing, learning to ride. She noticed their sensible clothes - tan jodhpurs; knee high English riding boots, and white shirts. In her hand-me-down tee shirt and jeans that really didn't fit, she didn't want anyone to see her.

Besides, oil city girls and Cajun girls don't mix.

Everyone knew that. That's the way it had always been.

With the town girls always looking so superior and whispering, "Isn't it a pity the way those Cajuns talk," while they spoke a language that only they seemed to understand. They had staked out this place for themselves and no one else could come in.

Now and then, Lapin lingered long enough to hear the riding master call, "Riders up!"

Perched on the fence, watching the class go through its drills, she dreamed of cantering in the riding ring or taking the low hurdles.

It was then that she first became aware of herself and unsure of herself. But there it was - eyes turned away or flickering when she walked past.

"Can't you see me? Can't you see me?" Lapin realized that for some people, she simply did not exist. She had reached too far before, and had paid the price. Heart broken, overlooked.

It was during those moments that she closed her eyes and let wonderful sweet memories flood over her.

* * * *

She was back in the convent school with Momma. Her mother worked there, earning enough to pay the small tuition for Lapin to attend.

Momma had always insisted that Lapin would have a Catholic school upbringing, as was the custom of aristocratic Creole families for generations.

But Momma's family had fallen on hard times. Wealth was just a memory, and she had to do whatever was necessary to see to Lapin's education - washing, ironing, or working in the kitchen.

Her Creole pride made her demand a great deal of liberty when she wasn't working.

She devoted her free time to Lapin, teaching her the old customs, the old songs, and showering her with tenderness.

Carmelite nuns educated Lapin along with the other children who lived there; some creamed colored, or yellow or brown. And just as her mother wished, the convent school education was aimed at training girls to be moral and religious. The children droned their lessons, and said their prayers, not paying much attention to the meaning.

Lapin and her mother were given cozy quarters upstairs in which to live. In the evenings, both in fresh cotton nightclothes, Momma sat rocking, Lapin in her lap. They talked in a soft Creole patois, with Momma filling Lapin's childhood fantasies with stories of her ancestors from Martinique.

It was a time of unutterable sweetness.

Sometime Lapin noticed the gardener, leaning on his hoe, watching Momma hang the clothes on the line. Now and then he gave them things from his barrow - tomatoes, strawberries or carrots.

During the passing months, Momma's steps had grown slower as she made her way up the steps each evening. It never occurred to Lapin that one day, Momma would be gone.

When she died, Sister Margaret Mary wrapped Lapin in tender arms, and did the next most perfect job of loving her. But the sadness that came with the cruel parting from her mother would be with Lapin all of her life.

Lapin continued in the convent school, and was given a roommate down on the main floor.

Whenever Lapin caught sight of the man from the garden, watching her, he quickly picked up his tools, turned away and busied himself. Did she only imagine that he looked at her with the anxious eyes of someone who loved her?

Now and then Lapin found fresh berries and primroses at her door, newly washed, draining on a paper towel, wrapped in newspaper.

Several months after she left the convent, Lapin learned that the gardener went away on a fishing boat that never came back from the sea.

Making friends at the convent had been easy. Everybody needed everybody.

There was plenty of love to go around. The nuns saw to that. Of course, everyone took turns settling for second best when it came to clothes or books. One day it was your turn and the next day, someone else's.

The convent girls had little differences between them in need, and none of the girls noticed the differences between them in looks.

Some had silken hair so fair that it was almost white.

The smallest had bouncing red curls and a face covered with freckles.

When Lapin, the oldest, read a storybook to her, the

little red head pushed Lapin's bronze fingers out of the way so that she could see the pictures better. Grabbing Lapin's arm, the little one would turn it over and over, looking for freckles like hers.

* * * *

A horse whinnied in the stable. The memory was gone and Lapin, still peering through the riding stable fences, into the dressage ring, snapped back to the present.

Suddenly she wanted to be as far away as she could get.

Does it matter? Do they care? Of course it matters. Of course they don't care.

No one noticed when she slipped quietly away and hurried on into the woods. In no time she'd be back in her airy loft in the little house in a clearing behind the hedgerow.

It's not that Lapin's life was full of drudgery. But knowing there were some things she would never be a part of, it wasn't worth it to try anymore.

Things changed when Maury came to the Hurst Stables.

Chapter Three

Best Friends

One Sunday morning in early September, Lapin was on her way home from the small Catholic Church on Kaliste Saloom Road. During the mass, she said her Rosary and even burned a candle to St. Jude, the patron saint of hopeless causes. She liked dipping her hands into the holy water, feeling the Rosary beads in her fingertips, whispering the old prayers again, and being a part of the church rituals. Sometimes Lapin sat in the same pew with the Carmelite nuns from the convent in Lafayette. On the days she got to sit next to Sister Margaret Mary, she felt especially peaceful and was certain that someone was hearing her prayers.

After mass, she walked her usual route past the Kimball's gate, down the road, and across the bridge over the coulee. She walked beside the white Hurst Stable fences up to the paddock area, dragging a stick in the dirt behind her, sometime clattering it against the slats in the fence.

When she got closer to the barn, she saw a lone girl working in the stable area. She had not seen this girl before. From the looks of things, the newcomer had just arrived. Things were piled up and scattered about.

Lapin leaned over her usual place on the fence, her fingers gripping the top rung as she edged closer to watch. She could hear the horses nickering and Maury clattering in the barnyard.

Maury was thinking about the things that she had to do when she finished grooming her horse. Clean the stall and load hay into it. Arrange the tack. Carry feed sacks.

At first, Maury didn't see Lapin. It was mid-morning, already hot and steamy. She was brushing down Blue Chip with her finishing brush, shining his dappled gray coat. She looked up to wipe her forehead with the back of her arm and caught sight of the girl looking at her.

She was perched on the top rung of the fence that surrounded the lot behind the barn, feet hanging. Maury saw the girl quickly turn her eyes away, and make a quick move to get down.

"No, wait." Maury called, walking toward the fence. She held out her hand.

"Come on over," she said.

Lapin, eyes widened, looked at the open happy face of this girl who was working a rubber band around wheat colored hair. She took Maury's hand, timidly at first. Then hung on for dear life as Maury pulled her down on the other side and helped her to her feet.

So a friendship began that would last a lifetime, though

the events of that autumn almost put an end to it.

"I could use some help." Maury spoke first.

"Sure," Lapin answered, smiling back. And for once she didn't go babbling on. It was always a problem figuring out when people wanted to talk and when they didn't.

She said only, "I haven't seen you here before."

"That's right. I just moved my horse out this week-end." Maury said as she reached

into a chest filled with crushed ice and cold drinks. "What's your name? I'm Maury Legé."

Getting out two frosty cans, Maury popped them open, handed one to Lapin, and leaned back against the stall door.

"My name is Lapin Doucet," the girl answered, reaching for the can.

Maury was glad to get a rest, and sighed as she looked up with pride at the new sign, which was already hanging there. 'BLUE CHIP' was engraved in the varnished wood. It hung on a chain from a nail driven into the stall door.

Maury, open, robust couldn't tell exactly why right now, but sensed a mystery in this olive skinned stranger.

No one said anything for a moment. Then Maury said, "Hey, want to take this saddle blanket and put it in the stall? I'll carry the saddle."

" Okay. But will they care if I go in?"

"Of course they won't care. You can poke around all you want."

They rummaged around a bit, rearranging things.

Then Maury grabbed a bag of chips. "I'm hungry. How about some?" handing Lapin the bag.

The girls looked at each other and settled down in the dust and straw, talking easily, like old friends, as it sometimes happens when you least expect it.

"Do you come here often?" Maury asked.

"No, I don't know much about horses." Lapin wanted to make a witty remark, but couldn't think of one. There was no need to tell Maury how often she had stayed out of sight when she walked past this place.

"Never mind. I'll teach you," Maury said, draining her coke. "Come on."

Lapin stood looking around. She took in the horse stalls, the hayloft, and the owner's small office.

Their stories went on, while the afternoon rain clouds began to gather.

"There's a lot to do here. Will you come back?' Maury asked.

Looking at Maury as if she might be joking, she answered, "I'll come everyday." She was triumphant.

Maury laughed and said, "Only if you want to."

"It's the most fun I've ever had."

A little while later Maury's dad drove up in the four-wheel drive. When she climbed in beside him, Maury looked out from the window and said, "Don't forget about tomorrow."

"Don't worry, I won't." Lapin replied.

Forget! Forget! How could she forget?

On her way back to town, Maury told her dad about the little girl and how sad her face seemed.

"Maybe she's lonely, " he said.

This was puzzling to Maury. She never worried about

friends. She'd always had them. And was quite sure that she deserved them.

Lapin watched the tail of the car until she couldn't see it anymore. She stood and looked around, and could hardly bear to leave.

There was so much to think about. She only knew that she would come again the next day, the day after that, and all the days that followed. But right now she had to run up the road and tell Mamere the news.

MaMere was waiting with supper when Lapin ran in the house. She sat down to eat, breaking cornbread into a bowl of milk.

Cheeks flushed, Lapin chatted away about Maury.

Lapin was rarely late, but Mamere was pleased. While they washed up the supper dishes, Mamere asked, "Goin' tuh see huh agin' tomorrah?"

"Oh, yes."

As she closed her eyes that night, Lapin thought, "This was not a dream. It was real."

Later, when Mamere went into the little girl's bedroom to say goodnight, Lapin's eyes were closed and she was sleeping soundly. Mamere bent to adjust the covers, and thought she saw a slight smile on Lapin's lips. She tiptoed out without making a sound.

The next morning, Lapin opened her eyes and sat up in bed. It was the sunniest morning she could remember. After breakfast, she ran through the woods, toward the stables in a world that was suddenly nicer.

Mamere stood at the window and watched Lapin run across the clearing. She made the sign of the cross. She hoped this new friend was not like the fickle mockingbird, whose song could never be trusted to be the same from one day to the next.

Unfortunately, Mamere couldn't stop the events that were about to occur.

* * * *

There was no question about it. Maury knew everything about horses.

"Let me get this straight," Lapin said, looking at Maury for guidance as her fingers worked each day with the buckles and straps.

She fed and exercised Chip, eyes darting around for Maury's approval.

Maury showed her how to use the grooming buckets supplies - body brushes, currycombs and hoof picks. When saddling, Lapin learned not to girth a horse too tightly. Soon she didn't bounce around in the saddle so much.

Sometimes the two girls worked quietly, side by side, in the barn, mucking out the stalls, spreading fresh straw about, or polishing tack in the show boxes.

On rainy days they lay in the hayloft trying to find a spot where a barn board was missing and a ray of sunlight might shine through.

They talked about things that were new to each other. They talked about how grand it was to have this place, and swore to be friends forever.

Lapin wondered how anyone could get along without

Maury for a friend. Maury, blustering through life as usual, was happy a new friend had fallen in her lap.

But most of all, they rode. Both astride the great gray horse, they flew through the fields, around trees, scattering the red and gold leaves. They found more wonders than anyone could imagine. They rode in the mornings, blinking back the sun's rays. They rode in the late afternoon, through lengthening shadows.

They feasted on sandwiches, chocolate bars, and sweet ripe blackberries that they picked themselves.

The days were perfect. They were best friends.

Chapter Four

First Visit

One day Lapin went home with Maury. Maury's mom picked them up after school.

Lapin wanted to act just right, and look her very best. On the ride over, Lapin remembered how she had twisted and turned for Mamere to inspect her.

"You'll be jus' fine." Mamere said.

Lapin hadn't been into Lafayette very often and didn't have much to say while they drove through the quiet tree shaded streets of Maury's subdivision. She looked at the curving cement driveways and green lawns, automatic sprinkler systems hissing cool water on the yards.

They pulled up in Maury's drive. It was wide, lined with azalea bushes and bridal wreath and cut a white slash through the St. Augustine grass. Maury's dad was standing at the barbeque pit in the back yard and gave his usual friendly wave, turning the chicken halves over.

"Look at your dad." Lapin said, pointing.

"What about him?"

"He's waving at us."

"My Dad never met a stranger." Maury said proudly.

They jumped out of the car, skirted around a huge magnolia tree, and grabbed a rib off of the pit. The smell of the smoke followed them into the house.

The girls threw their book bags on a table in the den, where floor- to- ceiling windows were open to catch the breeze. Lapin looked around. It was a friendly house, substantially built of white brick. The back yard was rimmed with pine trees. Large potted plants staggered up wide brick steps.

The two headed for the kitchen. Then took their snacks down the wide hall and flopped on chairs in Maury's room.

Maury slid a movie in the DVD player and they settled down.

Lapin thought it must be wonderful to live in a house like this white brick, full of books, enough furniture for every room and a closet big enough to play in. It was even close enough to school to walk, if you wanted to. You would never leave it, if you lived in a house like this.

After supper, the streetlights were coming on and night sounds beginning when Maury and her Dad took Lapin home. Lapin was quiet. Whatever she was thinking, her face was hard to read.

She was thinking about the house she lived in with her Mamere.

It was an old cottage in a clearing behind a hedgerow on the far edge of the Kimball Farm. Lapin wasn't exactly ashamed of her home. It might have seen better days, but it was always scrubbed clean and was big enough for the two of them. And there was always more on the table than they needed.

The original owners of the land had given Mamere the right to live on the property until her death. So when the Kimballs bought the acreage, Mamere came with it.

Lapin didn't mind that she lived with Mamere. She loved her.

Sometimes Mamere got out the old photograph album, and flipping through the pages they laughed together about happier times. There were faded pictures of assorted cousins, aunts and uncles. Lapin's favorites were the ones of Momma when she was a little girl.

Momma was buried in the Catholic side of the Old Crowley Cemetery, where great statues of stone rose among the tombstones, keeping vigil over the dead. It was shortly after she said good-by to Momma there that the nuns had begun to search for Lapin's relatives.

It had been a long time since Mamere had anyone to remember things with. The people she had done things with were all gone now. Looking at the old pictures, Mamere 's mind could reach back further than her dimming eyes could see.

This childhood home gave Lapin a sense of belonging somewhere. She knew that she was being taken care of, and always would be.

With Lapin there, Mamere didn't have time to think as much about her own children, who had been long gone from the isolation of the bayou.

Mamere was a legend - a wrinkled old traiteuse, who had been practicing voodoo for as long as anyone could remember.

If you wanted to ward off evil, bring the eyes of a frog to Mamere. If you needed to cast a love spell, bring black grapes and honey to Mamere. It wasn't any wonder that Lapin picked up some of this hand me down sorcery. In fact, it was the custom for an old traiteuse to pass the secrets to a younger person.

However, should she die without an heir, the secrets would die with her.

The old woman swore to uphold the tradition of the secrets that had come with her bloodline in the first years of American slavery. It was their only heirloom. It was all they could bequeath.

Everyone knows that left - handed children, like Lapin, have special powers. And early on, she learned how to use the voodoo, conjuring, and the power of suggestion. However, as it turned out, Lapin would come to wish that she didn't have such a vivid imagination.

Chapter Five

Mamere

Maury's first visit to the little house in the clearing came a few weeks after the two girls met.

Lapin had never invited anyone over before. She had never wanted to before. But she was feeling more and more sure of things. She didn't even think it was strange that Maury liked her.

One day, while they were brushing Blue Chip down, Lapin said quietly, "If you'd like to come over sometime…. I mean, it would be okay....". Her voice trailed off.

And once again Maury made Lapin feel ten feet tall.

She grasped Lapin's small hand firmly and said, simply, "I'd love to."

Two days later the girls met at the riding stable. Maury was waiting, Blue Chip tacked up. They mounted and headed to Lapin's house for shrimp gumbo and cracklins. They rode down a canebrake, through rows of sugar cane stalks, as tall as Blue Chip's head, then into the woods beyond the cane field.

They hadn't gone far into the woods when they came to the little house in the clearing. Maury tied Blue Chip to the fading wooden fence that encircled the small yard. Maury let her thoughts wander away for a moment, to stories she had heard about Mamere. She was prepared for any shock, but hoped it wasn't a bagful of spiders.

But just in case, didn't she have a dime around her neck on a string to protect her from gris-gris?

The cypress house was unpainted. Wooden shutters covered the windows. A stairway on the porch led up to Lapin's lodgings in the roomy attic. A steep roof overhung the porch.

Maury glanced at a thinly curtained window, and saw someone moving behind it.

Maury and Lapin, hand in hand, ran up the steps. Too late now. For a moment, Maury hoped the door wouldn't open.

Mamere stood in the shadows of the verandah. Taking Maury's hand, Lapin drew her closer to the form.

"Hello, my cheres,' Mamere said softy, smiling down at their upturned faces.

Maury walked up and stood beside Mamere. She found herself looking up into a kind old face; skin the color of bronze, framed in gray hair.

Maury blinked and stared a moment, her voice caught in her throat.

"How could this be?" she wondered, - this gentle-faced apron-clad granny.

After all, she had heard the stories about Mamere. Didn't she catch bad children and pop them into a sack?

Of course, Maury shouldn't be too afraid of Mamere. She had also heard funny stories about her. Maury's favorite was the tale of Mamere and the pop-bugs.

The story goes that almost every morning Mamere sat in a rocking chair out under an oak tree in her front yard. It was whispered that she was having a vision. But the truth was she usually had potatoes to peel or beans from her garden to snap. If she was lucky, someone from the boats down in Abbeville brought her and Lapin an ice chest full of fresh shrimp to peel and eat.

Whatever chore needed doing, her favorite place to do it was under the shade of that old oak.

Likely or not, sometimes she did it with a small glass of sugar syrup and rum nearby.

Sometime she just smoked her pipe and rocked. With her head leaning back against the chair, she looked up into the tree and pretended not to notice the children peeping out from behind the bushes on the edge of the woods.

She sat with one hand propped atop of her walking stick, one hand free to pull off the big black horned beetles, which crept in and out of the bark of the tree trunk. The older kids were on to Mamere, so they sent only the youngest ones over.

When Mamere saw that the kids had crept within hearing distance, she'd mutter, "Well, ah'm finished rockin', so ah think ah'll pick me some beetles fo' suppuh." With yellowing old-lady fingernails, she peeled the bugs off the tree and gave them a squeeze.

The bugs made a popping sound, legs quivering, curling and uncurling. Screeching, she batted them down, and the bugs scurried every which-way, right onto the sneakers of the stampeding group.

"You better get out of there." someone back in the woods would holler. "Don't go near her. She's horrid."

The whole bunch scattered, screaming in terror. Of course, they couldn't wait to come back another day with new victims.

And Mamere, putting her cold pipe in her pocket, leaned on her cane and laughed all the way into the house.

Snapping back to the present, Maury smiled to herself, and she and Lapin went inside. The door opened into a simple room. A good fire burned in the small hearth. Nothing was hiding in the shadows. The gumbo was simmering on the stove. The smell of the spicy brew and hot bread baking filled the house.

A large cypress side bar stood next to the fireplace. On a shelf, shiny things reflected the light from the glow of the hearth flames. There were small flat glass containers of ground seeds and leaves. One shelf was packed with jars of different sizes and shapes. Lying there were dried flowers and herbs, cornhusks, and knotted strings. Maury saw small loose seashells, black-eyed peas, and from what she remembered from Mardi Gras celebrations, something that looked like gris gris bags.

The floors were wooden, darkened by the years. The Kimballs kept Mamere supplied with her favorite tobacco. And the house was stained with the smoke from the pipe that she smoked.

In the dining nook, sun shining through a small stained glass window painted the table with color and brought life to the chipped crockery.

Mamere, an old Creole, spoke half French and half English as she put rice in the bowls and covered it with shrimp and okra gumbo. They broke a loaf of crusty French bread apart and dunked it in their bowls while they ate.

Mamere said, "You know, you cain't be nobody's friend, 'til you eat wid' em."

"My mom says the same thing," Maury answered, sensing right away, an unexpected opportunity.

Wiping her mouth with a paper napkin, Maury said in a most cunning voice to the old lady, "Could you tell us some things about the voodoo spells?"

Old, but not easily tricked, Mamere brushed her off with, "Rubbish." And dismissed it with a casual wave.

Lapin kicked Maury under the table.

Knowing right away that she had pushed it far enough, Maury thought while she ate her gumbo, "There would be no getting of secrets from the old lady, friendship meal or not."

While the girls were stacking the dishes, Mamere stood, back to the fire, and glanced at Maury. Her eyes shifted to Lapin and she saw color in the little girl's cheeks and the twinkle in her eyes.

A feeling welled up and touched Mamere's heart. It was then that she decided to give a part of the only thing she had to offer.

Moving away from the fireplace, Mamere fingered her shell necklace and said, in an off-hand manner, "Give me a stran' of yo' hair, Maury."

Removing the empty gumbo bowls from the table, Mamere took them into the kitchen. Before returning to the table, she stopped at the side bar.

Maury yanked out a strand of her hair just as Mamere returned with a black-eyed pea cradled in her palm. With her nimble old fingers, she tied the hair around the pea.

While she worked, she said, "Lapin will plant dis unduh huh window. When the pea sprouts, yo' friendship will grow."

As she had many times before, Lapin gazed at Mamere, bewildered. Was she really telling the secrets? Voodoo spirits must be powerful, or else how could Mamere know what Maury's friendship meant to her.

While they visited, the blaze from the fireplace cracked. Now and then the logs shifted, sending sparks up in a spiral, warming the little house.

Then Mamere shared a few not-so-secret voodoo mysteries with the two girls. She told them that a talisman carved in wood attracted friendly spirits. She explained that voodoo dolls could be made of wax, or wood or clay. She said that, yes, it is true, gris-gris bags were red was because that was a favorite color of the spirits

Suddenly, the stained glass window clouded over and the wind began to blow. Limbs tapped and scratched against the walls. A Louisiana rain, rumbling up from the gulf, was coming in.

Mamere and Lapin knew you couldn't go anywhere in these rains. Once they started, they could go on for hours. So all you could do was just sit on the porch and watch the drops tumble from the sky, hit the hardpan and bounce up again before the dirt turned to mud and soaked all the way to China.

Maury, too, knew what was coming. She had been caught before in a stinging curtain of rain, Chip's hooves throwing water up from the trail. She hurriedly got ready to leave, while the sound of the howling wind and the chiming of a clock agreed that it was time to go.

Unexpectedly, just as Maury was leaving, Mamere bent down and pulled her close.

Wondering how long the rain would hold off, Maury waved good-bye from atop the horse. She turned to look back and saw Mamere walking the quarter mile to her mailbox, black cape billowing in the wind of the coming storm. She was waving her walking cane in the air, swiping at the chickens. Or was she waving at invisible things?

Maury escaped into the autumn thunderstorm.

Chapter Six

Betrayal

Maury and Lapin were a team. A little magic settled on them.

Until the day Maury's plans changed.

Maury thought her explanation was simple and to the point. She was invited to move her horse from the expensive Hurst Riding Stable to the Kimball farm across the coulee. It didn't make any sense not to accept the offer, what with the Kimballs offering to keep Blue Chip there at no charge.

Both of Maury's parents worked and there was enough money, but they certainly didn't need to spend it foolishly.

Maury's parents had become acquainted with the Kimballs. Everybody was happy about the whole thing.

But it didn't sink in with Lapin. In a matter of minutes her life had changed.

* * * *

On the day of the move, she was waiting at the stable when Maury and her Dad drove up in the Jeep Cherokee, horse trailer attached.

So it was true.

Lapin ran into the barn, straight to the second door on the left - Chip's spot. She looked around at the empty stall. Blue Chip's sign was gone. The other horses were there, heads hanging over their doors. She felt suddenly sick, with a sadness that showed on her face, the kind she couldn't hide.

She ran back outside and turned to Maury. "Why are you doing this?" She was slightly hysterical. "I thought we'd be friends forever."

"And we will be." Maury answered. But she saw Lapin's face and tried a little harder. "Oh, come on, Lapin," she sighed, "I've explained it. You don't understand."

"No, I don't," she broke in.

Maury started to talk again, but Lapin heard only parts of it...."Time for a change".

"...Time for a change?" Lapin thought.

Maury tried to put her arm around the little girl. But Lapin pushed her away, barely listening now. They were already a million miles apart.

"Oh, to heck with it." Maury thought, as she whistled Chip in from the field, and led him up the ramp into the trailer. She could already see herself leading him down again onto the Kimball farm.

Maury quickly said good-bye, gave a little wave, turned

and stepped up into the Jeep. With her dad behind the wheel, she rode away without looking back, her head already filling with new thoughts.

Why was Lapin so upset? After all, hadn't they been watching the noisy riders at the Kimball farm from far back in the fields? And hadn't they both caught sight of Kevin Kimball, jaunty, blond hair shiny in the sun, cantering along the far fence?

"What do you think of him?"

"Isn't he wonderful?"

Maury remembered the evening, just at dark, when they crept to the edge of a stand of oaks and climbed through the fence. The soft murmur of voices reached them through the trees. The Kimball riders! There, fingers laced through the branches, they watched when the group turned off their flashlights and formed a secret society, whispering, "Friends forever."

And Maury thought again, "Wasn't it amazing that she'd soon be with them?"

Why should Lapin interfere with what she wanted most? She was on a precipice; something wonderful was going to happen.

"Oh, well. I'll sort it out later."

Maury was confused, but easily decided that this was not a day for worrying.

Seldom had she been so wrong.

* * * *

Lapin watched Maury ride away and wept. How can you have a best friend miles away? She watched the Jeep disappear, this time for good.

She could hardly believe she had done it again. She had wanted too much, and paid another price. The hurt crept through her body, and she became even a victim of her own thoughts. "Stop it. Stop it," she moaned, squeezing her head between her hands.

She had wanted to cry out for Maury to understand. But how could she? Maury would be like all the others, never knowing how it felt to be left out, somehow always finding a way around the loneliness.

And so it had been easy to slip into the old ways again, masking her feelings. Enough hurts, enough times, and you become good at it.

She closed her eyes, pressed her lips into a thin line, and thought, "It's Kevin. It's Kevin; he must have his hand in this. Yes, of course. That's it."

Lapin sat on a rock, thinking, for a long time after the car disappeared. She began to cry softly. Though she tried not to be heard, her wretchedness echoed through the trees, nowhere and everywhere.

A breeze blew the leaves around her feet. She lifted her face to the sky, and heard the whispers again, the voices of her ancestors, coming in the wind.

Lapin rested her chin on her knuckles, eyes narrowing, and said to the breeze, "But he is just a silly boy." Then she stood, her hands clinching into fists at her sides.

And at some unknown point she began her plan.

When she got back to the little house, Lapin banged

around in the kitchen, muttering. She was too big now to throw herself in Mamere's lap and sob.

MaMere couldn't make sense of it and continued sweeping the floor, carefully pushing the dust into a little pile, waiting. She saw Lapin's trembling body, and wanted to hold her close and stroke her hair. She wanted to say the right thing, but how could she find the words? How could she ever find them? Mamere only knew that Lapin's high spirits were gone. She was someplace Mamere couldn't go.

Throughout the next few days, Lapin stayed close to Mamere, more interested than she had ever been before, in her secrets. She followed Mamere on her trips into the woods for plants and roots and bog moss. She hovered nearby when the cupboard doors were opened and Mamere got the things she needed from the shelves of dry leaves and seeds. Lapin was never satisfied. She had no time for dalliances.

Chapter Seven

A New World

Not even twenty minutes had passed after she left the Hurst Stables, when Maury and her dad arrived at the Kimball farm.

Being the oldest and most responsible of the six Kimball brothers and sisters, Kevin met them when they pulled into the barnyard.

Dad and Mr. Kimball got Chip settled in his new paddock area.

Kevin turned to Maury and said, "Come on. I'll show you around." He grabbed her hand.

His eyes looked even bluer up close. Not that she was interested in him.

"That'll be terrific." Maury answered. She felt great.

Kevin showed Maury the horse trails on the farm. They toured the barn, tack room and other outbuildings.

As they rounded a corner, back at the barn, Maury said, "Wait a minute, Kevin."

She saw Craig Kimball tether his horse to the cross ties in the wash rack, then wash him down with a soapy sponge. Maury had done it a hundred times and knew what came next. She and Kevin stopped and watched as the boy hosed the horse down, just as he would a newly washed car. Then he ran his hands down the horse's legs, to check the hooves.

Un-tethering the horse, Craig gave a friendly wave and watched as his brother and the new girl headed farther into the barn to saddle up.

Maury and Kevin rode down to the Vermilion River, which backed up to the Kimball property. They stood on a levee and looked down at the water. It lay flat and still. A pirogue bobbed at the water's edge. Kevin pointed out a blue heron gliding below the tree line. The sound of a powerboat drifted from somewhere beyond the oak and cypress trees. Later this would become one of Maury's favorite places to come alone.

One by one she met the other riders. There didn't seem to be a place in the woods or bayou that one or the other hadn't been. They all had stories to tell. And in the listening, Maury became a part of the group.

The farm routine was established before Maury got there.

The kids stacked wood. Now and then something needed a coat of paint. Or a paddock post needed replacing. The riders did chores around the farm as part of the bargain for keeping their horses there.

They kept the horses groomed. If the stable vet wasn't

needed, they did their part to keep the animals well.

Craig's horse got sick the day after Maury got there, sweating heavily, twisting and rolling with colic. The boys were discussing the best way to deal with it.

There was no time for discussion anymore. 'Let's get him up quickly." Maury said.

She helped move him, as he snorted and yanked against the tethers. Maury told the others what to do, and took her turn walking him late into the night.

With a smile of triumph when it was over, she gave Craig a sisterly squeeze, went home and fell into bed.

It's not often that things are perfect. But Maury knew that this time most certainly was. Everyday grew more golden. Oh, the things that happened those days, when every path they took was filled with new things. They didn't need a reason to be happy. This was their world.

The best part was the riding. Early mornings, as soon as you could bridle, the ride was on. No waiting to saddle- the first one on the trail swiping away freshly spun spider webs clinging to his cheeks.

But no matter- they rode over the levees and into the pond, eight or ten at a time, where the horses splashed in, heavy bodies sinking. The riders, hanging onto the horses' mains, floated over their backs, ready to be in position to remount when the horses emerged on the other side.

On one cool October morning, they decided to drift down the bayou. Amidst a tangle of fishing poles and coolers, the gang went on foot into the shallows on the edge of the swamp. Frogs and long-legged insects leaped before them when they reached the thicker marsh grass.

There was no need for motors on the narrow wooden pirogues waiting in the reeds.

Maury and Kevin, shoulders brushing occasionally on the narrow path, were last to arrive, and got the last boat.

"Jump in, Maury." Kevin said. "I'll push."

Crawling in, he pushed the slim boat adrift with a long pole, through the cattails and water lilies, which nodded in their wake. They floated down the slow-moving bayou, which didn't seem to want to keep its rendezvous with the sea.

Maury closed her eyes and relaxed in the warmth of the sun. It was a mild windless day. The silence was interrupted only by the occasional shrill cry of a hawk, and water lapping against the sides of the boat. She and Kevin talked softy, fingers touching, not needing anyone else.

But the other pirogues were nearby and it wasn't long before Craig hollered, "Let's eat."

"Next time we'll come on our own." Kevin remarked. "Just the two of us."

Pulling the boats against each other, they tied the front ends together with old nylon ropes. They handed drinks, sandwiches and bags of chips around in a circle.

A whispering breeze carried the sound of their laughter to somewhere deep in the woods.

Someone was listening.

Something set the birds off.

A sudden breeze blew Maury's hair across her face, and rocked the narrow vessel. She felt a chill, goose bumps crawling up her arm. It was time to pole to shore and haul the boats out of the murky water.

Chapter Eight

The Threat

"Catching a snake is easy." Kevin said
"But you can't." Maury was horrified.
"I can."
"You're crazy."
You never knew when you were going to need a snake.
Especially when you wanted to make Spida-Ida squeal.

Ida, the twerp, was an easy mark - a nosey untidy girl,
always up on her studies, prancing around, thinking she
knew everything. A mop of spidery hair kept creeping out
from under her baseball cap.

Maury caught on pretty easily to snake – catching. If
you walked along the shallows of the marsh, and watched
your footing, you could usually see snakes curled up along
the edge. Of course, you had to know the difference
between a water moccasin and the harmless king snake.

But with a two-pronged stick, you could easily trap the

king's head in the prong. Then it was simple to grab it by the back of the head and throw it in a saddlebag for use with Spider-Ida later.

It was bad luck if you got caught. There was nothing Spida-Ida liked better than getting everyone in trouble. She'd fly through the bramble bushes to Mrs. Kimball, who immediately put a stop to snake hunting for the day.

Spida-Ida, who, as you may have guessed, wasn't as dumb as she looked. Sometime she crept along behind the snake hunters and grabbed the closest muddy ankle. When everyone finished shrieking, and weren't feeling nearly so superior, she gloated all the way back to the barn.

Sometimes, when she saw Ida sitting alone on the steps of the Kimball's big farmhouse, twisting her baseball cap in her hands, Maury secretly hoped that Spida Ida had a friend of her own somewhere in the world. Not enough, of course, to take the pledge to leave her alone.

You could keep a snake as long as you wanted. But an hour or two was usually enough.

The days fell into a happy pattern. Maury hardly missed Lapin. Or if she did, she didn't admit it.

In the late afternoon, when the sun was red and hanging just over the marsh, riders returned to the barn. They finished with the horses, cooling them down slowly, giving them water and hay. Then settled on bales of hay, drinking sodas, talking quietly. It was that magical end of the day, when even the birds were quiet and things stilled themselves.

The children waited for parents or big sisters to come and get them. And when they were gone, as if it had been waiting for them to leave, the sun dropped below the horizon and night fell over the farm.

From back in the swamp, in dense marsh grass and a tangle of growth that had never been cleared, someone was watching them all.

* * * *.

On an ordinary afternoon when Maury's mom came to pick her up, Kevin walked her out to the car.

Just as Maury was about to climb into the red Oldsmobile, Kevin laid his hand on her arm and said, "I'm glad you're here."

His eyes fixed on her face, and Maury couldn't think of a reply. She felt as eager as a raindrop waiting to fall and couldn't still her heart. All the way home, she kept her hand on the spot on her arm that he had touched.

One night, soon after, Kevin called Maury at home. She was working at the dining room table. Putting aside her homework, she reached for the portable phone in her mother's hand. She listened in silence, drumming her fingers on the table.

After a moment or two, Maury said, 'Yes. I'll be there after school. Wait for me if I'm late." Then she heard a click on the line and a dial tone.

Maury didn't explain anything to her parents. But the wrinkle on her forehead was unmistakable when she put the telephone back in its cradle.

She took her Coke and went to the kitchen. She stood

there drinking, looking out of the window as if an answer might come from out of the darkness.

"Anything we can talk about?" Her Mom asked.

"Not yet, Mom."

* * * *

Kevin went to St. Michaels's Catholic School in Lafayette. Maury's public school was across town. So there would be no time to talk with him during the day. The next afternoon, Maury's Mom dropped her off at the farm.

The Kimball home was set back a half mile off the road. But Kevin, still in his school uniform of navy slacks, white shirt and crested tie, was waiting in the shadow of an oak tree near the cattle guard at the entrance to the property.

Kevin saw the car drive up. Maury opened the door and jumped out. Kevin thought about all the afternoons of the past few weeks that he and Maury had shared. Each of them running out after school was over, to be together. As soon as he saw her easy smile, he knew he had made the right decision, telling no one else about what had happened last night.

Kevin waved Maury over. Taking her hand, he said, "We'll ride a bit by the river." She walked with him in the chilling afternoon air to the barn, where he had the horses tacked up and ready to ride.

They made small talk as they rode out of the barnyard. After a few minutes on the trail, Maury asked, "How much farther is it?"

"We're almost there," Kevin said.

During his phone call the night before, Kevin told Maury that he had something he needed to show her, and that he didn't want to talk about it on the telephone.

"Here's the place. This is where I saw the feu follet." Kevin said, as he dismounted in a swampy area in the woods.

"The feu follet? You can't be serious!" an astonished Maury answered, as she looked around.

Maury had heard the stories for years about this nocturnal non-being, the bayou "Will-o-the-wisp". This light seen hovering over marshy areas and cemeteries that had been blamed for countless tricks in the bayous.

"But did you really see anyone, Kevin?" she asked.

"No, not really. But I saw the light. I know it sounds crazy." A frown creased his forehead. "But I saw it. I saw it. I saw the light."

Kevin's gaze became remote.

"And then?"

He went on. Kevin explained that when making his usual routine trip to the barn just before bedtime, he discovered the barnyard gate open, swinging in the wind. He was certain the gate had been locked. Somehow Black wandered out of the barn and the gated barnyard. So he had gone out deep into the woods the evening before, looking for his horse.

When Kevin caught up to the horse, he had hardly found his way home. Even those most familiar with the bayou know the danger of being lost in its murky blackness. The bayou kept its secrets.

A chill swept over Maury, as Kevin continued.

He pulled on Black's reins, as he led him back. Here in the woods, in the dark, the wind, which had started almost as a whisper, seemed stronger. It's wail, louder. His nerves were now on edge and he couldn't shake off an uneasy feeling.

Kevin thought he heard something. He glanced around. "Anyone there?" He called out.

Black jerked his head toward the sound, almost pulling the lead rope from Kevin's hand. Then he saw it - the light flickering in the marsh. He stopped and looked toward it. Kevin recognized it as the light twinkling from the windows in his barn. It was late, and walking straight toward the light would be a shortcut home.

He followed the glow, but didn't seem to make any progress. The path was covered with thick overgrowth. But Kevin thought he must have been getting close. And he started toward the barn again. Then he stumbled and stopped short. He was back where he started. He had been walking in circles.

Where was he? Which way had he come?

Then he saw them. Fresh tracks. Someone had been here.

He thought he heard the sound of someone near - a breath, a rustle, a twig snapping under a shoe. Was someone there? Was it his imagination? Whatever it was disappeared in a bank of fog.

Still frightened, Kevin shivered and the misty light suddenly disappeared. And just as unexpectedly, he stumbled upon the path that had led him there. He followed the trail home. It was one, which he had traveled many times before. He knew all it's twists and turns.

"This is a longer route." He thought. "But I can follow it clearly." He began to walk faster, still leading his horse. As he made his way back, he saw familiar landmarks.

Craig Kimball stood at the large kitchen window watching as his dad swept the beam of a flashlight across the yard that separated the barn from the house. Mr. Kimball headed toward the woods, continuing on to the first fork in the trail and on to the next. He saw the big black first, moving through the shadows. Then Kevin.

"Kevin! Here, son!"

"Dad! Dad!"

With his dad's arm around his shoulder, Kevin was glad when the barn came in view.

"Kevin, we're here." His mother shouted, from her position at the barn gate. Kevin saw the lights and heard the dogs barking. He went through the barnyard, knowing they would all have questions. Questions he could not answer. Once inside, with Black back in his stall, his sense of well being returned.

"Wow!" Maury exclaimed.

She could hardly believe it. And, for once in her life, she was almost wordless. She was a girl who preferred to deal with facts and hard evidence.

They walked together, leading their horses, neither of them saying a word.

Then, sounding a lot more confident than she felt, Maury said, " Kevin, you don't have to tell anyone else what happened."

"I won't." His voice quavered. Kevin was feeling foolish and embarrassed at his own chatter.

Then Maury smiled and said, "But I'll tell you what I know about getting rid of a feu fottet. If you think you are being conjured, just cross your fingers and spit three times."

Kevin turned to Maury, his face pale and bewildered.

That did it. Maury couldn't hold it any longer. She smiled up at Kevin and they both fell over in a laughing fit.

Then Kevin sighed and said sheepishly, "Maury, there's been some other trouble."

"Trouble. What kind of trouble?" Maury's breath caught in her throat. "Go on."

"It makes no sense." he continued.

"A few nights ago something woke me up. Something has been spooking the horses and I haven't been sleeping well."

He went on, "I saw it in the moon's light, a shadow on the porch. But by the time I got to the window, it was gone. And I found this on my window sill." He drew a small rag voodoo doll out of his pocket.

Kevin didn't tell Maury that he felt fear hanging in the air that night and that he dropped to the floor by the window. He had heard the sudden fluttering of startled birds. Something told him, don't move. Don't get up. He knew there were places in the lush shrubs surrounding the porch where something could creep dangerously close, hide and wait. Someone had been there. He could feel it.

"Oh, brother. Great, just great." Maury thought, feeling

a sudden chill. She knew, suddenly, who was behind it.

This was more than a prank. Attempts to laugh it away now stuck in her throat.

They were almost back at the barn now.

"Kevin, the person who put the doll there believes that power can abide in any object," she said. Leaning closer to him, she whispered, "But you and I know it's just a rag doll. Will you trust me to deal with this? I might know who is to blame."

Kevin thought Maury was maddeningly calm. But he agreed.

It was clear in her mind, and though there might be trouble ahead, Maury knew what she had to do.

Chapter Nine

Reunion

In another part of the woods, in a shack, in a clearing, Lapin lay on her bed remembering the things that happened a few nights before.

She had edged away from Kevin, dowsing her small torch in the swamp. Then she began to run madly through the unruly swamp grass, her heart pounding in her chest.

"Hurry, hurry," she thought, as her bare feet flew though the field separating the woods and the little shack. Not slowing, she headed toward the dim light coming from the upstairs window of the little house, ran up the steps, stumbled through the open door, and slammed it shut. Sobbing, she grabbed her magic potions and hurled them across the room.

"What have I done?" She choked sobs into her pillow. "It's Kevin. It's Kevin. I hate him." But she knew that wasn't true.

She stared at the ceiling, barely lit by a misty moon, and thought about the reasons she needed a friend so badly.

Was it because of the color of her skin? She wasn't black. She wasn't white. She didn't belong here. She didn't belong there. She was no one. Should she wear her hair straight? Should she wear her hair curly? Should she wear a skirt? Should she wear jeans? Why can't I get it right?

She remembered the bus rides to school when the kids from town greeted each other with bursts of laughter, each wanting to be the first to tell what had happened since the day before. It was easy for them, exchanging secrets with each other as they made their way down the aisle.

Mostly, they just looked disinterestedly at Lapin, as if she wasn't there. In fact it made no difference if she was there or not. That was probably the hardest part.

Lapin could slip into a seat at a cafeteria table, hoping to start a conversation. The girls hardly looked at her. She kept her eyes downcast, but she could see them waving others over, or drooling over some boy.

Leaving the tables in the lunchroom, they broke up into groups of three or four. She would still be just one. The way they huddled together, someone must be saying something funny, something perfect.

Mamere always told Lapin to study hard and do her homework. She could always do anything with Science, and wondered why everyone else found it so difficult. She was called on a lot. But still no one noticed her, and brushed by her, hurrying to leave after class.

Always calling out to someone else, but never to her, "Wait for me. I may be late tomorrow."

Keep walking. Keep smiling. Dig in your book bag.

And while she remembered, the tears fell out of the corners of her eyes, rolled down her cheeks, and dropped silently onto her pillow.

* * * *

It had been easy for Lapin to slip out of the house and dash out into the night. She could creep down the stairs that led from her upstairs room and follow them down to the bottom, where they ended on the veranda. The rest was easy. She knew these woods like the back of her hand.

It was on such a night that Lapin made her way to the Kimball home and crouched in the shadows. Kevin's room was at the edge of the porch. No lights were on in the house. She drew in her breath, crept up the steps and took a rag figure from the red bag around her neck. She placed it on Kevin's windowsill. She began to sway in a circular motion. And in a voice so low that only she could hear, she began a chant to the spirits. When it was done, she fled into the woods. Squawking birds rose from the trees.

* * * *

Soon Maury neared the hedgerow by the little house in the woods. She was through searching through the past when she dismounted. It was time to make things right again.

"Hello. Anybody home?" she called out as she tied her

horse to the cypress fence. She hoped the sight of her wouldn't make things worse.

Lapin had slept fitfully. Fully away now, she walked to the window, moved the curtains slightly, and gazed through the clearing toward the hedgerow where Maury was approaching.

She heard Maury's call.

When she didn't hear any anger in Maury's voice, she shoved her feet into a pair of sneakers and pulling a tee shirt over her head, slipped into her jeans. She opened the door a crack and stepped out, just as Maury reached the bottom of the porch steps.

Lapin glanced back over her shoulder and closed the door softly behind her.

From another part of the house, Mamere heard the door open and close.

"It will soon be over," she thought.

"Lapin, we have to talk." Maury said, not certain she could say the words that could make things right between them again. But she knew she had to try. She had to help her friend out of this thing.

Lapin tried to swallow the lump in her throat. She fought against the sobs that were threatening, and said, almost in a wail, "I'm sorry." realizing that Maury knew what she had been doing.

Maury blinked back the moisture that was forming in her eyes, and, reaching for her little pal, said, "Oh, Lapin, I'm sorry, too."

For the first time, looking at Lapin's twisted face, Maury realized the harm she had done. How could she have let her down? Nothing could match the regret Maury was feeling now, but she had to think only of what must be done. She put out her hand again and Lapin met her half way.

"It's all right," she said; as she reached down to wipe the tears away from Lapin's wet cheeks.

If Lapin ever had a wish, it had just come true.

"Wait here Maury." Lapin said, and she ran back into the house.

Maury sat down, relaxed and leaned back against the steps. Through the screen door she heard the refrigerator open, the tear of cellophane from a carton. Lapin came back with Cokes and sweet rolls.

The girls sat side by side on the steps, feet in the dust, the great oak bent over them.

The magic, or whatever it was, was back. It happened gradually, and they were back in it before they realized it, or even understood it.

"Not a bad pair, are we?" Maury asked.

"Not bad at all."

Lapin tried to explain to Maury just how it was. She was tired of pretending that it didn't matter. It did.

"Maury, I don't know if I can tell you."

"You can tell me anything."

And she told Maury all about it at last.

They talked about everything, and finally they talked about school.

Lapin said, "Its not as if they say anything. It's just that they act like they don't know I'm there. But I didn't mean for it to go this far. I really didn't."

"I didn't realize how it was." Maury answered. "But you're too smart to keep on with this. You are something stronger, something better. You don't have to prove anything."

Lapin sighed – better, stronger? Let it be true. Please make it be true.

Remembering the friend she had once been, Maury vowed, "But if you really want me to, I can help you. After we finish, you won't be just someone they see at school. I promise."

"I promise, I promise....". The words kept spinning around in Maury's head. How often had she heard her mother say, "You will be judged by the promises you keep."

Chapter Ten

The Feu Follet

On the night of the cochon de lait, Maury had her chance to keep her promise.

The day dawned cold, signaling a perfect night for a bonfire.

The gathering for the pig roasting had begun early in the day.

It was to be held down by the oak tree that the Kimball's had fenced off for large outdoor parties. Kimball parties meant that everybody came, lugging lots of food, and gathering by a huge fire. It might be a crab boil or a fish fry, almost anything that was in season.

But tonight there was to be a cochon de lait - a pig roasting. The young hog would be roasted all day slowly in the open over hot coals, and basted with homemade sauce.

They pig would be cut into halves and each portion

suspended from a metal hook, that let the meat turn while it was being roasted.

The smoke from the fire floated up slowly into the air, and the smell of the pork cooking could be detected throughout the farm. It drifted over to the little shack in the clearing, where Maury and Lapin made their plans.

Mamere, also invited to the occasion, was stirring her jambalaya in a large iron pot. Tangerines and figs, picked from trees growing near the little house, were already in a wicker basket ready to be toted over. Sugarcane, pulled from its stalks by Maury and Lapin, from atop Blue Chip, was tied in bundles. Later, it would be chewed for its sweet juice, the dried fibers then spat out.

At dark, when everyone began to gather around the glowing fire, sweet potatoes were baking there and greens were boiling with salt meat. Homemade deserts and salads lay out on checkered cloth covered tables.

Grownups milled around a shady circle of chairs, nibbling on shrimp croquettes.

The younger children, jars in hand, raced after lightning bugs, or took turns on the tire swing. Craig Kimball tossed softball from hand to hand, looking for a game.

The older kids gathered near the bonfire, some nuzzling closer than was necessary, arms around each other's shoulders. They waved greetings, and then went back to their whispering.

Someone threw a log on the fire. Sparks flew up and disappeared into the night.

And, as if on signal, Maury and Lapin emerged from the woods, once again together, astride the big gray horse.

On the morning of the cochon de lait, there couldn't have been anybody who didn't know that Maury was bringing a mystery guest. A guest who could talk about old voodoo powers and maybe work a little magic.

Now they saw her. They knew Lapin was the girl who lived with Mamere. They had seen her at school. Some of them had seen her at mass. But no one remembered seeing her anywhere else.

The girls dismounted. The hum of conversation died. Only the crackling of burning logs broke the silence. What moonlight there was, came in spurts as the moon slipped in and out of sight from an overcast sky.

Everyone watched Lapin lift a tattered bundle from Blue Chip's back. A whisper of a breeze stirred.

Lapin's black hair was tied with a red ribbon. A gold cross on a chain hung around her bronze neck. She began to twist it with trembling fingers. Maury reached over and touched Lapin's arm. The small girl quieted.

Then Lapin sat down cross-legged in the group of silhouettes, dark figures against bright orange flames. She looked up at the moon, rocked back and forth slightly, raised her hands up and out, then swept them in a circle and called the children close.

And so, it came to be that on an autumn evening, under a spreading oak, Lapin spun her tales.

She told them about the magic of frogs' eyes, hummingbirds' hearts, hoodoo bags and such. She talked of moon lore - dream of a wedding, hear of a death. Sleep in the moonlight and bring on madness. Bad luck will follow if you put a towel on a chair, or shoes on a bed.

She showed them good luck charms - a bore dollar, a knotted string. She reached over and tied one of these knotted strings around Ashley's small extended hand, winked, and said, 'Now you'll get rid of that cold." Ashley shot her a look of doubt.

Lapin glanced around and for a minute, and trembling slightly, wished she were sitting in her cozy bedroom. But she took a deep breath and went on.

She began the tales of healing powers. To remove a wart, say a prayer, circle the wart with a lighted match - not close enough to burn - and blow out the match

She told them only what Mamere agreed she could tell about the herbs that could be collected in the woods. Herbs that could be mashed or boiled and used for fevers or head colds. Or that could be made into plasters to rub on scratches and sores.

Lapin lowered her voice and they huddled closer. She shook her finger at them, and warned them about the wicked woman who lived on the banks of the Vermillion River. She swims the bayou, looking for bad children, whom she grabs and pops into a sack. Then she swims with them back to her hiding place in the marsh.

"I don't believe it." Ida grumbled. "And you're a stupid fool if you do."

"Shhhh." someone said.

Lapin, smiling, said, "I'm not sure I do either, but Mamere told me that her parents had used the threat of calling that wicked spirit to quiet many a rowdy fais doo doo."

Lapin reached into her pouch, drawing out small plastic

bags filled with beans.

Giving one to each child, she said, "Put these on the headboard of your bed. If the couchemar, the night visitor, slides inside your room one night, don't breathe. Don't move. It will stop to count the beans. This will keep it busy until morning. Then it will disappear with the sun's light."

Maury said, "Lapin, tell them about the love glove."

Lapin looked up at her. But Maury nodded and winked her on.

Lapin explained, "Well, you must steal a glove from the one you're after. Fill it with sugar and honey to sweeten his affection. Then sleep with it under your pillow. And anything might happen when you see him next."

And for the little ones sitting around the fire, Lapin had special tale to entertain them. Lapin placed a box of colored birthday candles on the ground and said, with drowsy music in her voice, "Select the color you wish. Close your eyes, rid your mind of all thoughts, and focus on your goal."

Eager hands reached into the stack of candles. Once lighted, the flames were set a dance in the breeze.

Raising her voice slightly, she went on, "Then chant:
' Special candle, flame, flame,
'There's magic in the color that I name.' "

When the candles were blown out, Lapin said,

"If you picked a yellow candle, happiness and success will come to you. If you picked blue, peace and serenity will be in you and around you." She drawled on, "A green candle will bring good health to you and those you love."

For a moment no one knew what to say.

Then Ashley asked, "But, Lapin, why do people believe this stuff."

"We believed it when we were little, before we were taught not to believe." Lapin replied. "It's not so different from people who simply believe in good luck and bad luck. Like we all throw salt over our left shoulder, knock on wood, cross our fingers, or step over cracks in the sidewalk.

Finally, looking across the fire at Kevin, she explained about the feu follet.

"You've all seen one, haven't you?" she smiled as she asked. "Well, it's dancing light is no more that the spontaneous combustion of gases caused by decaying plants. Just like we learned about in Science class."

"Most important," she said, "magic is all around you and in you. It can be around any corner, or behind any door. If you want something, keep saying it and believing it and it will be part of you. The magic will make it happen."

As the kids gathered around her she knew there was also magic in friendship

Finishing this last story, she looked up at Kevin. Couldn't he understand?

And as he stood there, he did.

Kevin had been swept away with the mystical tales. But magic could go just so far. He much preferred this real live girl. She was different, set apart from the others, but hopefully not from him.

Lapin looked around and knew that it was ending. She wasn't holding on by a thread anymore. She had really done it. She could look them in the eyes, feeling more confident, not so afraid that they wouldn't like her. It seemed easier to believe in fairness now.

After all, they weren't too perfect, too smart. And so what? It didn't really matter.

They were who they were. She was who she was. She could find the middle now. Taking what was good about people and skipping over the rest. Lapin hoped that they would do the same with her. Because people really don't change a lot, though Father Bertrand said that we could keep trying to make the best of ourselves.

Mamere had told her that voodoo was a simple and good thing, not something to be afraid of. And that it could bring healing between people. Mamere was right, again.

What had Lapin really wanted after all? Maury as a friend? She was glad she had that. It was still important.

But she had herself now, her private self. She could make her own way. She'd have room for a lot of things in her life. New things and things she thought she had left behind.

It would be enough to be back under the roof with Mamere, each taking care of the other. To find her favorite place on the hearthrug and sit by the fire with Mamere, where they never ran out of things to say, lapsing into French when they felt like it.

And to gaze out of her own upstairs window in that roomy attic, watching the leaf shadows playing under the limbs of the old live oak and Mamere's chair stirring gently in the breeze.

When up in her loft, safe in her bed, she could listen for the sounds of the floor creaking below, the screen door closing softly, and the muffled voice of another night visitor, in need of mystical potions.

Lapin looked around until her eyes fell on her friend, standing back a bit.

"Thank you, Maury," she mouthed. Maury returned a silent nod.

* * * *

Maury watched as the embers died and everyone was saying goodnight. There would be other nights, but this was a night they would remember. In fact, this was a night against she would measure many others.

Its funny the way things turned out.

Maury saw Lapin bend to gather her things. Then she saw Kevin move to Lapin's side, looking as if he wanted to be there a long time.

Lapin heard a voice behind her say; "I'll help you with these."

She looked up into Kevin's face when he took her hand in his. She made no move to pull away, and said, "Kevin, I have a lot to tell you." Her eyes were dancing.

Maury saw the look that passed between them. In those glances was a feeling Maury understood at once.

She looked at Kevin a moment longer and turned away. Pulling up her collar against the frosty night air, Maury hoped that somehow, one day, she'd stop seeing his face every time she closed her eyes.

"Maury, Maury. Come boost me up." Called the Kimball baby sister, the tough little tree-climber who usually followed them around.

As Maury boosted Shawn up onto her pony, she looked around at this place, lost for a moment in the sounds and sights of that night.

Instinctively she knew that her heart would forever be in Louisiana – this place-her place, forever green, where she rode fast across the fields and wandered slowly back. Where mornings could be so still, hot and wet, smelling of salt water. This place where sudden storm clouds gathered, rumbled across the sky, died and made way for the sun.

Until now, Maury had been busy thinking about tomorrow and the next day. And being with childhood friends was enough.

But something happened in that autumn of her twelfth year.

She thought about life going on. Starting high school next year, growing up, and leaving the bayou, maybe doing something important.

A brief wistfulness passed quickly, because Maury knew she would hold these memories in her heart forever, when she played out the last games of her childhood.

She understood that what you don't see is still there. Whenever she walked in sweet green grass, or heard rain drumming on a roof, she'd be home again. And as she traveled away from childhood, memories would be part of the journey.

If, in a time far distant, she were in another place, under another moon, that moon would bring her back full circle in memory to this place, this blessed place, as its beams bounced off a still bayou and through a stained glass window in a cottage behind a hedgerow in a clearing in the woods.

The clouds slipped away to another place in the sky. The night was bright again.

Maury's parents looked at this girl, their sweet young girl.

As Maury walked toward them, she heard the call of a lonely loon rise up in the darkened sky above the cypress trees, breaking the silence of the bayou.

Sometime during that winter, Maury and the loon swept out of the bayou on silent wings.

The End

Teacher's Guide

Have you ever been careless with a friendship?

Have you ever felt left out, or overlooked?

Are you more like Maury? Lapin?

Have you, or would you, make an effort to be friendly with someone who is different from you?

Is it okay for people to have different religious beliefs and still be friends? Why? Or why not?

How far would you go to win back a friendship?

Have you ever lost a boyfriend, girlfriend, to someone who was a close friend?

If you were having trouble with a friendship, would you discuss it with your parents, teacher, counselor?

How far would you go to be part of the crowd?

Classroom Activities

Divide the class into groups. Child selects area of interest.

Group A. Find books on voodoo and bring explanations, and, or, demonstrations to class.

Group B. Trace the history of the Acadians to Louisiana. Start in Europe, on to the new world, and through the United States.

Group C. Trace the history of the Creoles in Louisiana. Start in Europe, then into the French West Indies, and then to the United States.

Group D. Discuss the bayous of Louisiana. Plant life, animal life, dangers. Pros and cons of developing oil business on the coastal waters.

Group E. Make and serve gumbo. Use paper cups, a rice cooker, and readymade roux. (I recommend Bootsies, made in Louisiana, and available in most stores.) Using a hot plate, add boiling water to the roux. After sufficiently mixed, drop one shrimp for each child into the mixture and boil for five minutes.

Pronunciation Guide and Glossary – THE FEU FOLLET

Feu Follet – Fee- Fo –Lay (will of the wisp)

Lapin -- Lah-Peh

Doucet – Do-set

MaMere – Mah-mair (slang for Grandmother)

Traiteuse – tray-toose (someone who dabbles in voodoo)

Cochon de lait – coo shawn do lay (pig roasting)